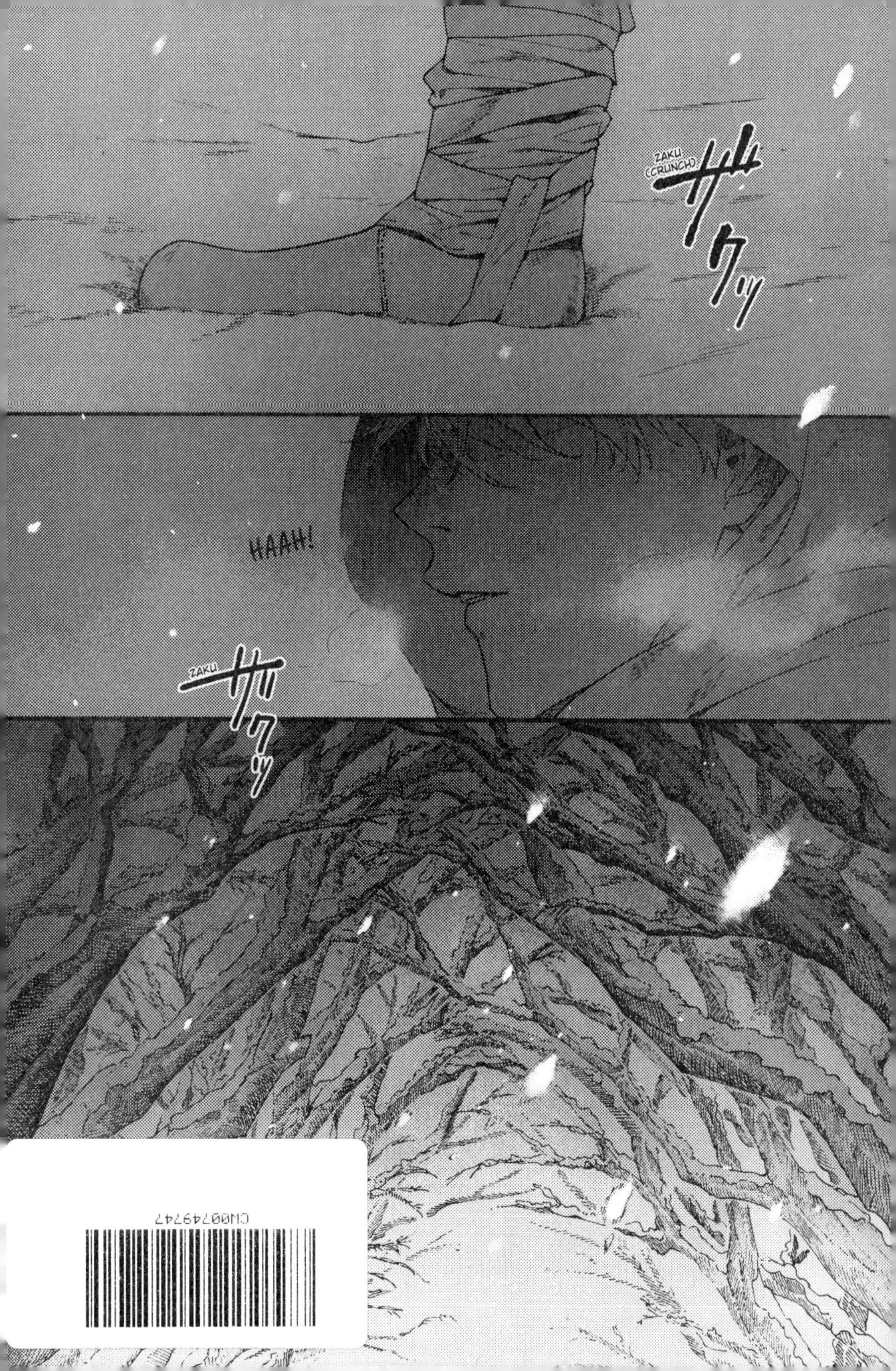
ZAKU (CRUNCH)
ザクッ
HAAH!
ZAKU
ザクッ

FURA
(WOBBLE)
GARI
(SKRITCH)
BOWA
(GLOW)

ふらっ
FURA
ふら
FURA
HFF!
HFF!
ガくっ
GAKU
(BUCKLE)

DOSA
(THUD)

GU (BLUB)
ぐっ
ぐっ
GU
PACHI (CRACKLE)
パチ
PACHI
パチ
GACHI (CHINK)
ガチッ
PACHI
パチ
PACHI
パチ

ほか
HOKA
(STEAM)
HOKA
ほか

うとっ…
UTO (DOZE)
こくり
KOKURI (NOD)
こくり
KOKURI
AH!
ガクッ
GAKU (JOLT)

KOPOPOPO (GLUP)
コポポポ
ポ…
KUN (SNIFF)
くん
KUN
くん
KOTO (TUNK)
コト…

ず!!
ZU
(SIP)

GUI (GULP)

SU (SHP)

GUGUI

SECOND CUP!

I'M COLD.

END

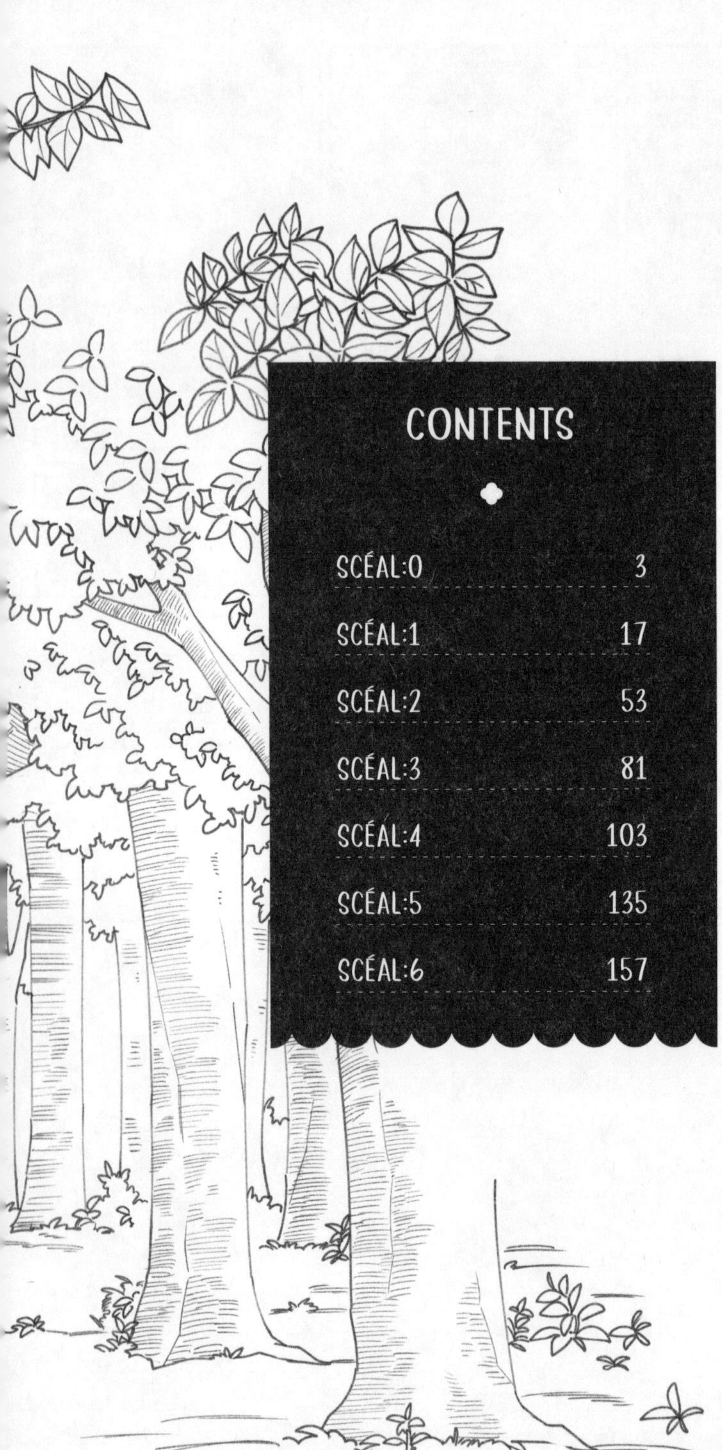

CONTENTS

Aria of the Beech Forest

ONCE UPON A TIME, IN A LAND KNOWN AS ERIN...
...MANY A WITCH MADE THEIR HOME.

THIS GIRL HERE IS NO EXCEPTION...

SCÉAL:1

HAAH!
SO MUCH SNOW...
HER NAME—ARIA. 
SHE RESIDES IN THE DEEPEST REACHES OF THIS BEECH FOREST.

ピタッ…
PITA (HALT)
DROPPED STITCH
NOW I HAVE TO START OVER...

I'VE NEVER SEEN IT PILE UP LIKE THIS BEFORE...
WHO WOULD'VE THOUGHT WE'D GET SUCH HEAVY SNOW THIS YEAR?
I WONDER IF I'LL NEED MORE LOGS...
I HEARD BEFORE THAT THEY DON'T USE FIREWOOD IN TOWN...
...BUT THEN, WHAT DO THEY BURN TO STAY WARM?
IS IT ME, OR...
...IS THERE SOMETHING... WRIGGLING? UNDER THE SNOW...?
うずい
UZU (SQUIRM)
...
UZU
うず

JUST IN CASE...

GIII-
(KREEAK-)

TO
(TNK)
トッ
TO
トッ
HYOKO
(PEEP)
ひょこっ

A WHITE...

... RABBIT?

JITO (STARE)

IT'S HARD TO TELL.

ZAKU (CRUNCH)

PIKU (PRICK)

MUKU (RISE)

BORO (POMF)

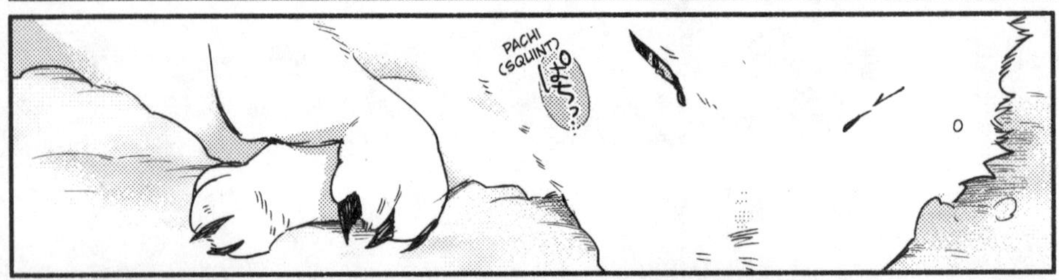

ばっ
BA (FWIP)
WHA—
WHAT DO I DO?
M-MY FIRST WOLF !!
FOR NOW, I'LL RUN INDOO—
もぞっ…
MOZO (SLINK)

!
ぱちっ
PACHI (SNAP)
ビクッ
BIKU (FLINCH)

むくり…
MUKURI

G-GET A GRIP, ARIA.
EVERY-THING'S FINE. I JUST NEED TO CALM DOWN.
スッ…
SU (SLIP)
YEAH. IT'LL BE OKAY. AFTER ALL, I AM...

BA
(FWIP)
...A WITCH!
DODON
(BABAM)
PURU
(TREMBLE)
PURU
WEAK-KNEED
B-BR—! B-B-BRING IT ON! I'M READY.........
SORRY, KID...
BA

I DON'T... MEAN YOU ANY HARM
THOUGH, UH...
GUGYURURU (GRUMBLE)
COULD YOU SPARE ME SOME FOOD...?
...I AM PRETTY HUNGRY.
AM I HEARING THINGS...?
WHERE'S THIS VOICE COMING FROM...?
...?
CAN YOU HEAR ME?

HERE YOU GO.
colcannon

COLCANNON IS...
A MASHED POTATO DISH MADE WITH CABBAGE AND KALE!

PERO (LICK)
ペロッ
KUN
KUN (SNIFF)
SORRY I POINTED MY WAND AT YOU BEFORE.
...

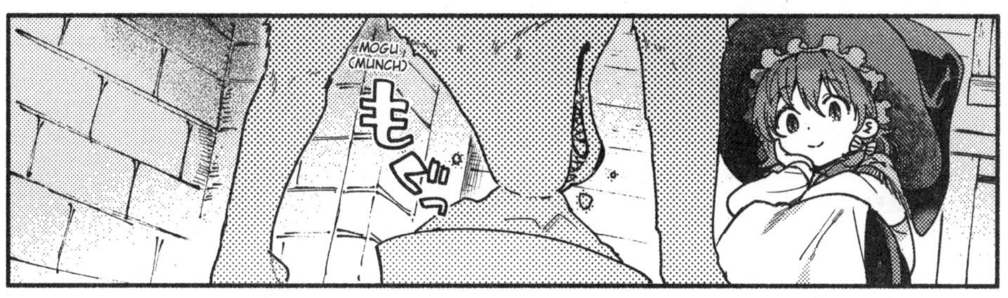
MOGU (MUNCH)
もぐっ

I DIDN'T REALIZE WOLVES COULD EAT POTATOES.
MOGU
MOGU
I EAT ANYTHING.
THOUGH I THINK YOUR STANDARD WOLF STICKS TO A MEAT-ONLY DIET.
WERE YOU...
...ABAN-DONED BY YOUR OWNER, MR. WOLF?

?

WHAT GAVE YOU THAT IDEA?

WHEN I TOOK A GOOD LOOK, I SAW HUMAN FOOTPRINTS NEXT TO YOU.

THAT'S WHY I THOUGHT IT MIGHT BE SAFE TO GET CLOSE.

...I SEE.

WRONG, THOUGH ...

SETTING THAT ASIDE...

...AREN'T YOU GOING TO ASK WHY I CAN SPEAK LIKE A HUMAN?

TSUN (POKE)

WELL SURE, I WAS STUNNED AT FIRST, BUT...

...I'VE HEARD ABOUT IT FROM MY GRANDMA.

SFX: PACHI (CRACKLE) PACHI

YOUR GRAND-MOTHER?
YEP!
SHE TOLD ME THERE ARE ANIMALS WHO CAN COPY HUMAN SPEECH USING MAGIC.

MY GRANDMA'S A SUPER-SPECIAL WITCH!
EVEN AMONG WITCHES, SHE'S A VEEERY BIG DEAL, AND SHE KNOWS TONS OF SPELLS.
I BET THAT'S HOW SHE KNEW ABOUT TALKING ANIMALS LIKE YOU, MR. WOLF.
HEH-HEH!
DOYA (SMUG)
HMPH.
GIKU (GULP)
YOU HAD A WAND EARLIER. ARE YOU A WITCH TOO?
W-WELL YEAH ...
...BUT I'M STILL TRAINING!
SO, UM... I'M NOT MUCH YET...
...BUT ONE DAY, I'LL BE JUST LIKE GRANDMA.
COLOR ME IMPRESSED.
...DO YOU LIVE ALONE HERE?

YUP.

THERE'S A MERCHANT GUY WHO DROPS BY EVERY SO OFTEN, BUT...

THERE WE GO!

...US WITCHES CAN'T HAVE PEOPLE FINDING OUT ABOUT MAGIC...

...SO I'M NOT ALLOWED TO GO OUT.

YOU'RE NOT?

SO YOU'VE NEVER LEFT HERE, EVEN ONCE?

? NOPE.

KYOTON (BLANK) キョトン

ANYWAY, THIS WAS THE FIRST CHAT I'VE HAD IN AGES!
...SAME HERE.
A TALKING WOLF...
...WOULD SCARE ANYONE, UNLESS THEY WERE A WITCH.

YOU...

KYUPIIIN (EUREKA)

...POOR DOGGY! YOU WERE ABANDONED 'COS YOU CAN SPEAK, WEREN'T YOU...!?

URU (TEARY)

URU

I'VE READ ABOUT IT IN BOOKS...!!

SHE'S MADE UP A WHOLE STORY AND WON'T TAKE NO FOR AN ANSWER...

"DOGGY" ...?

OH, WELL. I GUESS THAT WORKS FOR ME TOO...

IF YOU WANT, YOU CAN STAY HERE AS LONG AS YOU'D LIKE...
DAKI (HUG)
TH-THANKS...

YES.
GOOD POINT.
THAT MIGHT ACTUALLY BE NICE.
IN THAT CASE...
...WOULD YOU MIND LETTING ME STAY—JUST FOR THE WINTER?
HUH!?
SU-SURE.
OF COURSE!

......

YOU REALLY DON'T EAT PEOPLE?

I DO NOT.

AND THAT WAS HOW A LONE WHITE WOLF...

...ENDED UP FINDING SHELTER WITH A WEE WITCH, JUST FOR THE WINTER.

ピク
PIKU (PRICK)
ガタ ガタ
GATA (CLATTER) GATA
ザァァァ…
ZAAAA (WHOOOOSH)
ガタ
GATA
ガタ
GATA
ガタ
GATA
HEY...

WHAT'S YOUR NAME, MR. WOLF?
...I DON'T HAVE ONE.
YOU DON'T? DOESN'T THAT MAKE THINGS DIFFICULT?
I DON'T KNOW. I'VE NEVER HAD ANY ISSUES WITH IT.
I RARELY SPEND TIME WITH ANYONE BESIDES MYSELF.
PACHI (CRACKLE)
PACHI
PACHI
OH?

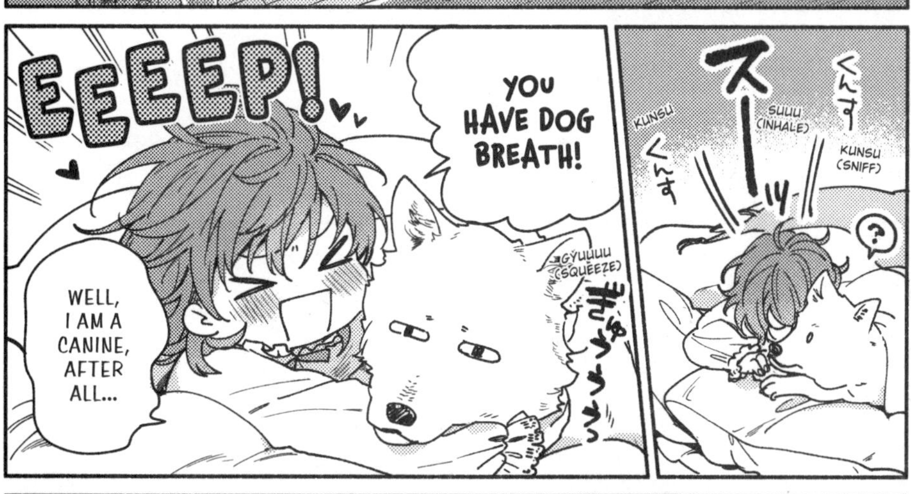
くんす
KUNSU (SNIFF)
スーッ
SUUU (INHALE)
くんす
KUNSU
?
YOU HAVE DOG BREATH!
EEEEP!
GYUUUU (SQUEEZE)
WELL, I AM A CANINE, AFTER ALL...

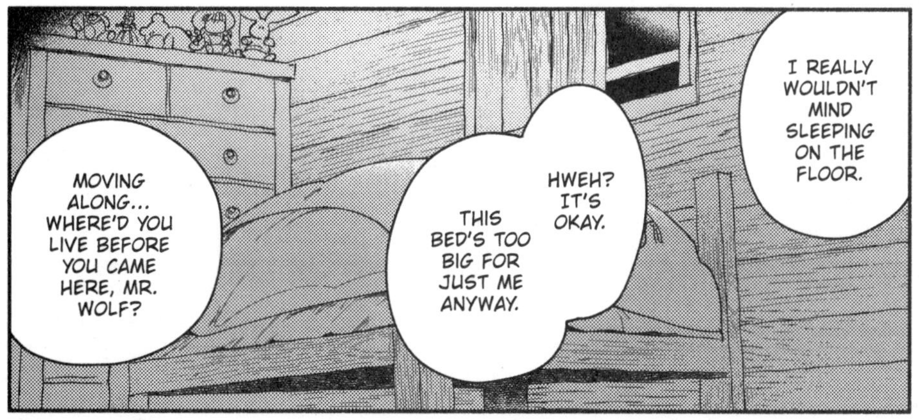
I REALLY WOULDN'T MIND SLEEPING ON THE FLOOR.
HWEH? IT'S OKAY.
THIS BED'S TOO BIG FOR JUST ME ANYWAY.
MOVING ALONG... WHERE'D YOU LIVE BEFORE YOU CAME HERE, MR. WOLF?

IT'S A LITTLE WAYS AWAY FROM HERE, BUT...
WAIT, NO.
I GUESS IT'S NOT ACTUALLY THAT FAR.
GEEZ. WHICH IS IT?
SO WHAT'S IT LIKE?
...GOR-GEOUS.
SO BEAUTIFUL THAT I SOMETIMES DOUBT IT WAS EVEN REAL TO BEGIN WITH.
ARIA...
DON'T YOU EVER WISH YOU COULD LEAVE MAGIC BEHIND AND GO LIVE IN TOWN?
UTO
HUH?
DID I EVER TELL HIM...
UTO (DOZE)
ARIA?
...MY NAME ...?
SUU (SNOOZE)

KUPIII (SNORE)
くぴーっ
KUPIII
くぴーっ
SHE'S ASLEEP...
GRAND-MAAA...
FUNYAAA (MURMUR)
ふにゃ〜…
GOOD NIGHT, ARIA.

HERE.

barm♥brack

ボトッ
BOTO (FLOOP)

ぼへ～～…
BOHEEE (DAZED)

IT'S SO NICE OUT TODAY.
I THINK WINTER'S ALMOST OVER.
I'M GLAD. PHEW!

じとっ…
JITO (STARE)
......?

HAAAAH...
A HUGE SIGH!?
!?

YUSSA
ゆっさ
YUSSA (SWAY)
ゆっさ

DOOON (BAM)
ドーーーン

...? WHAT ARE YOU DOING?
WHAT'S WITH ALL THE OMINOUS CURSING TOOLS...?
A SNOW-MAKING RITUAL.
KERO (BLUNT)
ケロ

N-NO, ARIA!
IT'S FINALLY STARTING TO GET WARM!!
B-BUUUT—!
ばっ
BA (WHAP)
WHY!?
YOU SAID YOU'D LEAVE WHEN THE WEATHER'S WARMER, MR. WOLF...
WAAAAUGH!!
MIND LETTING ME STAY—JUST FOR THE WINTER?
HIC!
HIC!
OH YEAH. I DID SAY THAT, DIDN'T I?
IS THAT WHY...?
...A LITTLE BIT BEFORE YOU SHOWED UP...
...MY GRANDMA DIED.
THIS YEAR WAS MY...
...FIRST WINTER WITHOUT HER, AND...
......

DON'T WORRY. THE SNOW-MAKING THING WAS JUST A JOKE.
YOU HAVE A PLACE TO GO HOME TO, RIGHT, MR. WOLF?
SUKU (RISE)
NOBIII (STRETCH)
ANYWAY! I THINK I'LL DO SOME MORE KNITTING TODAY!
ARIA...
I LOST MY HOME AGES AGO.
I HAVE NOWHERE TO GO BACK TO AND NO PLACE TO LIVE.

IF IT'S ALL RIGHT WITH YOU...
...I'D LIKE TO STAY HERE A LITTLE LONGER.

くいっ
KUI (YANK)
......
ぶんぶんっ
BUN
BUN (SWING)
??
しゅたっ
SHUTA (SWOOSH)
!?
GWYN.
IT MEANS "WHITE."
HOW'S THAT FOR YOUR NAME, MR. WOLF?

IT'S A LOVELY NAME.

SO WOLVES WERE HOW THEY STAY WARM IN TOWN WITHOUT FIREWOOD.
?
WHAT'S SHE ON ABOUT ...?

END

~How to Make Colcannon~

1. Steam the potatoes, and mash them until they're nice and smooth. Then add milk, butter, and salt, and mix it all together.

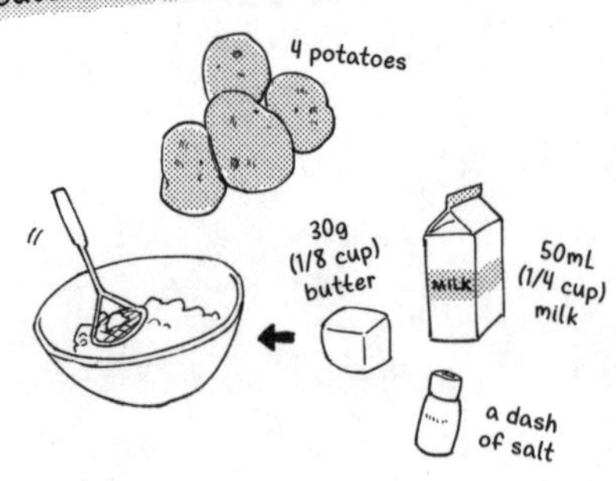

2. Stir-fry the bacon and cabbage.

Mix 1 and 2 together. Add pepper and parsley.

SCÉAL:2
......
NOTHING'S BITING...
BOOO (DURRR)

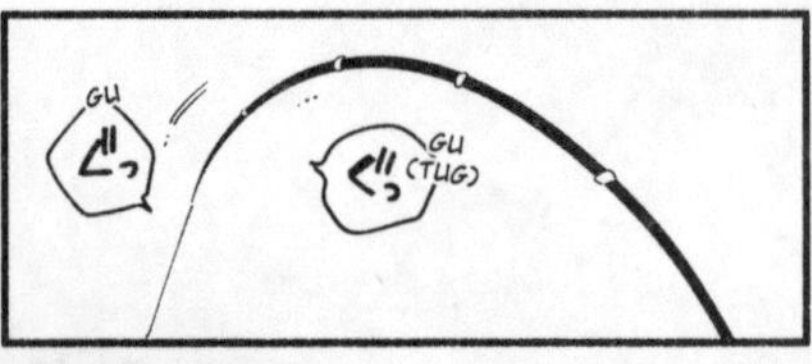

I GOTCHA NOW! DINNER!

GU ぐ GU ぐ…

WE'LL FINALLY HAVE SOME FRIED FISH ON THE TABLE TODA—

GYURU (CRANK) ギュル

GYURU ギュル GYURU ギュル

ZAPAA (SPLASHHH) ザパァ…

BORO (CRUSTY) ボロッ…

I COULDN'T CATCH ANY IN THE END...

I NEED A NEW SPOT.

ZAWA
(SWISH)

FUWA
(FLUTTER)

ZAA
(FSSH)

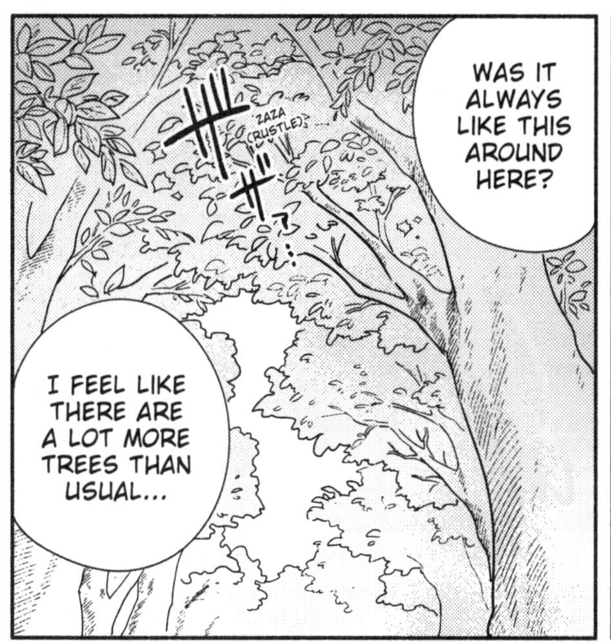
WAS IT ALWAYS LIKE THIS AROUND HERE?
ZAZA (RUSTLE)
I FEEL LIKE THERE ARE A LOT MORE TREES THAN USUAL...

...?

THIS IS MY USUAL FISHING SPOT, ISN'T IT...?
ZAA (BURBLE)
ZAA

...

ZAZA (RUSTLE)
JUST THE WIND...
GUESS IT'S LOUDER 'COS THERE ARE MORE TREES.
ZAZA
IT'S LIKE IT'S ALIVE. CREEPY, MAN...
MAYBE I SHOULD HEAD BACK BEFORE I LOSE MY WAY...
HYOI (PULL)
!...
HM?

OH, A PERSON...
PHEW!
WAIT, WHY'D I GO "PHEW"?
IT'S NOT LIKE I WAS SCARED OR ANYTHI—
BUN (SHAKE)
BUN.
DO YOU STILL NEED MORE?
WE ALMOST HAVE ENOUGH.
TWO...
KOSO (SNEAK)
A... GIRL? IN A STRANGE OUTFIT.
?

CHON (SIT)
ちょん
BUT IT'S PRETTY HEAVY. I DOUBT I CAN CARRY ANY MORE...
HOW ABOUT WE COME BACK AGAIN INSTEAD OF TRYING TO DO IT ALL IN ONE TRIP?
WE'LL BE FINE! I'M SURE YOU CAN HANDLE IT, GWYN!
!?
ARIA...
YOU MAY NOT LOOK IT, BUT YOU SURE DO WORK YOUR MEN (?) HARD...
IS THAT WOLF... TALKING!?
THIS MUCH SHOULD BE EASY FOR YOU, SHOULDN'T IT?
HAAH...
GYU (CINCH)
ギュ
I'M MORE WORRIED ABOUT THE BALANCE...

YOU KEEP COMING HERE TO COLLECT TWIGS FOR FIREWOOD, BUT...
...ARIA, CAN'T A WITCH LIKE YOU JUST SOLVE THAT WITH MAGIC?
SA (SLIP)
サッ
"WITCH"!? DID HE JUST SAY, "WITCH"!?

I MAY BE A WITCH, BUT I CAN'T JUST USE MAGIC WILLY-NILLY WHENEVER IT SUITS ME!
ASE (SWEAT)
あせ
WE NEED TO APPRECIATE MOTHER NATURE.
AND TO DO THAT, EVEN WITCHES MUSTN'T RELY ON MAGIC FOR THINGS THEY CAN DO WITH THEIR OWN HANDS!
IT'S TOTALLY NOT BECAUSE I SUCK AT MAGIC—I DON'T!
あせ
ASE
ASE
あせ
GYU
ギュッ
GYU
ギュッ
NIKOO (SMILE)
ニコォ。。。
WH-WHAT'S WITH THAT FACE...?

A... WITCH...?

OH, NOTHING. I THINK IT'S VERY VIRTUOUS OF YOU.
BY THE WAY, ARIA, DO YOU KNOW WHAT A LIGHTER IS?
NO, WHAT'S THAT?

JI (STARE)

WELL, SHALL WE HEAD HOME, THEN?
TOTA (TROT)
とた
TOTA
とた
WAIT UP, GWYN! DON'T JUST LEAVE ME WONDERIIING!

OH!

THIS IS NO TIME TO BE STANDING ARO—
THEY'RE ALREADY GONE!!
VANISHED

I KNOW I SAW THEM...!
GOKURI (GULP)
WITCHES REALLY DO EXIST...!
WHEE HEE
HEE HEE
HEE HEE!

THE TOWN?

WITCH?

THAT'S RIGHT.
HAVEN'T YOU EVER WANTED TO SEE IT?

BUT WE WITCHES HAVE RULES TO FOLLOW...
UMMM...
OH YEAH... WITCHES MUST CONCEAL THEIR MAGIC...

BUT THAT'S NO PROBLEM AS LONG AS NOBODY SEES YOU USING IT, ISN'T IT?
PAKI (SNAP)
POKI (KRAK)
... HMMM...
SHE WON'T GIVE ME A STRAIGHT ANSWER. I BET SHE JUST DOESN'T WANT TO GO...

OKAY, FINE. I WON'T PUSH.
THAT SAID, THIS PLACE ISN'T TOO FAR FROM WHERE OTHER HUMANS LIVE...
DO ANY EVER WANDER IN?
OH NO. WE'RE SAFE HERE.

BEAST...?
GRANDMA PUT UP A MAGIC BARRIER AROUND THE HOUSE...
...SO NOT EVEN BEASTS CAN GET IN EASILY, LET ALONE PEOPLE.
I... SEE...?
PAKI
パキッ
OH MY GOSH, GWYN! HOW DID YOU GET HERE!?
IT TOOK YOU THIS LONG TO ASK!?
SAAAA (PALE)
BORO (SPILL)
ぼろっ

AS I THOUGHT.
THERE'S A SCRATCH ON THE SIGIL THAT'S STOPPING IT FROM WORKING.
HMMMMMMM...

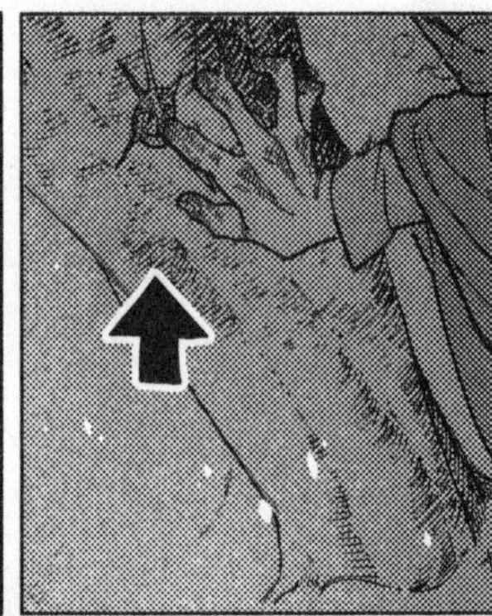

ARE YOU NOT ABLE TO FIX IT?
CULPRIT
TO TELL THE TRUTH, I'VE NEVER TRIED BARRIER MAGIC MYSELF...
MM-HMM...

GAKU (SLUMP)

...THOUGH THE STEPS SHOULD BE WRITTEN IN GRANDMA'S GRIMOIRE...
I SEE.
UNAWARE

※SEE SCÉAL:0

'KAY! LET'S GO HOME AND HIT THE BOOKS!
TEKO (TRUP)
TEKO
...

TEKO
TEKO
SO SHE WAS ALL ALONE INSIDE THIS BARRIER, HUH...?

GRANTED, ARIA DIDN'T SEEM TO CARE MUCH ABOUT THE OUTSIDE WORLD, BUT...
...I CAN'T HELP BUT FIND IT SAD.

THEN AGAIN, WHO AM I TO DECIDE WHAT'S BEST FOR HER?
?

※IRELAND'S PROFESSIONAL SOCCER LEAGUE

SFX: MOKYU MOKYU

?
WHAT DO YOU WANT?
GUI (TUG)
ぐい
GUI
ぐい

ぱあっ
PAAA (BEAM)
I BELIEVE YOU, BIG BROTHER!

...
MOKYU (MUNCH)
モキュ
MOKYU
モキュ
MOKYU
モキュ
MOKYU
MUSSHU (SLURP)
むっしゅ
MUSSHU
むっしゅ

HAAH...
?
MUNSHU
MUNSHU

IT'S A TOY SWORD, BUT IT'S BETTER THAN NOTHING.
GACHA (KACHAK)
OH?
ALVIN, HONEY, WHERE ARE YOU GOING?
FRIEND'S PLACE.

OH MY! YOU HAVE FRIENDS?

COME HOME BEFORE IT GETS DARK THEN, ALL RIGHT?

HEE HEE!

DUMB HAG...

...

I DIDN'T THINK IT WAS THAT FAR FROM MY USUAL FISHING SPOT, BUT...

ZAA (FSSH)

...THIS PLACE FEELS... CREEPIER THAN I REMEMBER.

ZAWA (SWISH)

ZAWA

NOW, I'M PRETTY SURE THEY WERE AROUND HERE...

THOUGH THERE'S NO WAY I'LL FIND THEM THAT EASI—

GASA (RUSTLE)

GASA

BIKU (FLINCH)

!

THEY'RE RIGHT THERE!!
ISN'T THAT DESIGN DIFFERENT FROM THE SIGIL WE SAW?
BUT THIS IS THE ONE IN GRANDMA'S GRIMOIRE.
SA (SHF)

SO I REALLY DIDN'T IMAGINE IT...
THE TALKING WOLF IS REAL!

IF I CAN GET A VIDEO TO SHOW MOM...

SFX: GOSO (RUMMAGE) GOSO

......

I WAS SO FOCUSED ON THE SWORD THAT I FORGOT MY DIGITAL CAMERA ...!!
ZUUUN (GLOOM)

HYOKO (POING)
ひょこっ
ZUN
ずん…
PA (BEAM)
ぱっ!!
B-I-G!
TA (TMP)
タッ
BRO! THEEERRR!

ZUKO (TRIP)
ズコッ
KOTEN (PLONK)
こてんっ
COLLEEN !?
AH!
OUCHIE...

WE...
WE'RE IN TROUBLE ...

OH!

FROZEN.
...
ピタッ PITA (HALT)

ARIA? YOU OKAY?
ちょい CHOI (SWIP)
YOO-HOOO.
ちょい CHOI

YOU WERE RIGHT! MR. WOLF CAN TALK!
SQUEE!
びしっ! BISHI (POINT)
I TOTALLY FORGOT!
GH CRAP!
ボケ～ BOKEEE (DAZED)
SQUEE!

GABA (LUNGE)
I KNEW YOU'D BE HERE, EVIL WITCH OF THE WOODS!!

YOJI (SQUIRM)
UM... UH...
AH... UM...
ER...
STAY BACK, MONSTER!
WITH YOUR STRANGE MOANING SOUNDS!!
JIRI
URK!
JIRI (INCH)
YOJI
??

GAAAN (SHOCK)
MONST—!?

OH NO...

THIS IS WAY TOO FUNNY...

MEGA-SURREAL...

KEEP AWAAAY!!

?

ER...

UH...!

NH!

AH...

TOY SWORD

ORO (FRET)

ORO

CAN'T COMMUNICATE TO SAVE HER LIFE

END

Henry
The vacuum cleaner
from Britain:
Henry

Sleepy...
Get up!!
SCÉAL:3
Howling
Growth...
Picking herbs

HERE YOU ARE...
KOTO (TUNK)
コト...
OH, THANKS...

MOJI (FIDGET)
もじ
MOJI
もじ

WAIT... WHY AM I HAVING TEA WITH HER...?
THIS TEA TASTES WONDERFUL.
HOKA (STEAM)
ほか
HOKA
ほか

COLLEEN! IT COULD BE POI-SONED!
DON'T JUST GO DRINKING THAT!!
?
GAAAN (SHOCK)
POISON!?

ABOUT THIRTY MINUTES PRIOR...

A TALKING WOLF...
...AND THAT OUTFIT...
YOU'RE A WITCH, AREN'T YOU!?
NOW THAT YOU'VE FOUND US OUT, OUR HANDS ARE FORCED...

WE CAN'T SIMPLY LET YOU LEAVE KNOWING OUR SECRET.
GRRRR...
JIRI (INCH)
ジリ…
SO...
...YOU ARE BOTH CORDIALLY INVITED TO ARIA'S HOUSE!

!?
WE'LL GO!!

...AND THAT'S HOW WE ENDED UP HERE.

CHOI (BECKON)

GWYN, C'MERE FOR A SEC...

WHY'D YOU BRING THEM HERE!?
WELL, I DIDN'T THINK LETTING THEM RUN STRAIGHT HOME WAS THE BEST IDEA...

YOU "DIDN'T THINK" IT WAS THE BEST IDEA!?
OH, WELL, UH...I WAS WORRIED IT'D SNOWBALL INTO SOMETHING BIGGER...

THERE'S NO WAY TALKING WOLVES EXIST IN THE HUMAN WORLD...
...SO IF HUMANS FIND OUT ABOUT ME, THERE'S A POSSIBILITY THEY'D TAKE ME AWAY AND EXPERIMENT ON ME.
WHAT!?
NO!! I'D NEVER LET THEM TAKE YOU AWAY, GWYN!
だきゅっ...
DAKI (HUG)
GYU (SQUEEZE)
ぎゅ...
MOFU (FLUFF)
もふっ...
I DON'T WANT THAT EITHER... WHICH IS WHY YOU MUST DO THIS FOR ME, ARIA...
YOU HAVE TO BE FRIENDS WITH THEM.
"FRIENDS" ...?

LISTEN. ONCE THEY'RE YOUR FRIENDS, THEY'LL BE IN THE PALM OF OUR HAND.
THEY WON'T DARE TELL A SOUL BECAUSE THEY'LL FEEL A MORAL OBLIGATION TO PROTECT US.
"MORE-UL OBBLY-GAYSHUN"?
IT MEANS THEY'LL FEEL BAD FOR US.

...

FUKI (WIPE)
FUKI

ARE YOU UP FOR IT, ARIA?

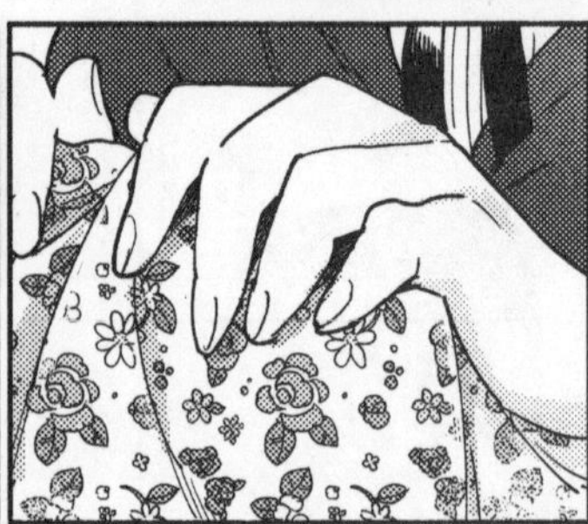

KYU (GRIP)

IT'S OKAY.
I CAN DO THIS. I'VE BEEN DOING MORE THAN KILLING TIME THESE PAST TEN YEARS.

I HAVE THE KNOWLEDGE GRANDMA LEFT ME IN ALL HER BOOKS—

THAT'S RIGHT! I READ SOMEWHERE...

...THE KEY TO MAKING FRIENDS...

...IS...

もっきゅ MOKKYU (MUNCH)

むぐ MUGU (CHEW)

もぎゅ MOGYU

もっきゅ MOKKYU

むぐ MUGU

...TO PAY CLOSE ATTENTION TO WHAT THEY'RE SAYING AND SHOW THAT YOU'RE A GOOD LISTENER!!

KURURI (TURN)
くるり

But how do you get them to start talking in the first place...?
HOLY CRAP...

Wh-what else was there? Uh...opening up to them, was it?
Open up about what, though!?
Easier read than done...
HER SOCIAL AWKWARD-NESS IS MORE CRIPPLING THAN I THOUGHT...
I WAS NAIVE...

もっきゅ
MOKKYU (MUNCH)
もっきゅ
MOKKYU
もきゅ
MOKYU

......?
YOU DIDN'T PUT ANYTHING IN THE HALLOWEEN CAKE?
?

AT MY HOUSE, THERE ARE RINGS AND COINS IN IT.
YOU EAT RINGS AND COINS!?
yum-yum
BARI (CRUNCH)
BORI (CRONCH)
BUBUUU (BZZT)
NOOOOO!!
IF YOUR PIECE HAS MONEY IN IT, THAT MEANS YOU'LL BE RICH.
AND IF YOU GET ONE WITH A RING, YOU'LL GET MARRIED.
Barmbrack
A traditional Irish fruitcake served on Halloween. What you get in your slice tells your fortune for the year. Apart from rings and coins, there are items like rags (poverty) and sticks (an unhappy marriage), etc...
IT'S JUST A SILLY SUPER-STITION.
......NOW THAT YOU MENTION IT THOUGH, IT'S NOT EVEN CLOSE TO HALLOWEEN.
DRINKING THE TEA, AFTER ALL
ZU (SIP)
AND THE TEA'S WEIRD TOO.
"W-WEIRD"...

THIS IS, UM... NETTLE TEA...
NETTLE? YOU MEAN THOSE POKY LEAVES?
IT'LL STING ALL DAY IF YOU TOUCH THEM...
(SCIENTIFIC NAME: URTICA)
NETTLE
An herb with pointed hairs containing venom. Should not be consumed raw or even touched, but is great for health, as it has antibacterial properties and can improve blood circulation!!
MAMA SAID NOT TO TOUCH THEM 'COS THEY'RE DANGER-OUS...
...BUT I DIDN'T REALIZE YOU CAN MAKE TEA WITH THEM!
YOU CAN USE THEM FOR COOKING TOO.
I PUT THEM IN OMELETS AND SOUPS...
...ALL THE TIME...
?? WHY'S SHE ACTING SO SURPRISED ...???
WOOOW!
DRYING OR HEATING REMOVES THE SPIKY HAIRS!!

YOU KNOW SO MUCH ABOUT HERBS...
NO WONDER YOU'RE A WITCH...!
ぶわっ
BUWA (BLUSH)

CAREFUL, COLLEEN. SHE'S GONNA FEED US LOTS OF TREATS AND THEN EAT US UP WITH A SIDE OF HERB MARINADE.
NO FEAR AFTER REALIZING ARIA'S HARMLESS
PAKU (NOM)
HYOI (HUP)
YOU'RE GONNA EAT ME?
OF COURSE NOT!!

OH, PLEASE! THAT'S WHAT WITCHES DO. THEY FATTEN UP KIDS AND EAT 'EM.
I KNOW THAT STORY! IT'S "HANSEL AND GRETEL."
MAMA READ IT TO ME BEFORE. ♥
YOU SHUT UP, COLLEEN!

I'M STARTING TO THINK WE SHOULD DEVOUR THEM JUST SO THEY'RE NOT DISAPPOINTED.
NITA (SMIRK)
NOT YOU TOO, GWYN!
QUIT STARTING TROUBLE!!
'KAY.
KARAN (CLINK)

TIME TO GO HOME.
WHAT!?
SUTA (STAND)
AWWW.
I WANNA KEEP TALKING WITH THEM...
PUUUU (POUT)
I'M THE ONE ALWAYS GETTING YELLED AT FOR BRINGING YOU OUT OF THE HOUSE.
GET HOME TOO LATE, AND THE OLD LADY'S GONNA BE MAD.
H-HOLD ON A SEC!
I CAN'T LET YOU LEAVE!
BA (LEAP)
?
WHY NOT?
BECAUSE WE HAVEN'T BECOME FRIENDS YE—
OH! I MEAN, UM...
"FRIENDS" !?
WHAT THE...?
!
"FRIENDS"!

とこ
TOKO (TRUP)
とこ
TOKO
ぎゅっ…
GYU (GRIP)
!
MISS WITCH...
...YOU MEAN YOU'LL BE MY FRIEND?
HUH!?
UHHH...
KOKU (NOD)
KOKU
KO
KOKU
KOKU
KOKU
...YEAH.

YAAAY! CAN WE COME OVER AGAIN!?
GYU
UH...!??? SURE, WE'RE FRIENDS, AFTER ALL......???? ?????
YIPPEE!
SO DUMB. AS IF I'D COME BACK.
LET'S GO.
UUUGH!
SEE YOUUU!
I'LL BE BACK!
OH...! UHH...
D-DON'T TELL ANYONE ABOUT GWYN, ALL RIGHT!?

...DO YOU THINK THEY'LL KEEP OUR SECRET?
WE'LL BE FINE.
NO WAY THEY'LL KEEP THEIR MOUTHS SHUT, BUT NOT LIKE ANYONE WILL BELIEVE THEM......
COULD SHE BE SOMEONE YOU'D SAY IS LIKE A "FORCE OF NATURE"...?
ARE WE REALLY FRIENDS NOW? AAAARGH! I HAVE NO IDEA HOW THIS STUFF WORKS...
ENJOY IT. AREN'T YOU HAPPY SHE SAID THEY'D COME AGAIN?
HM? YEAH...
BUT I'M FINE IF THEY DON'T...
SOWA (FIDGET)
SOWA
THAT HOPEFUL FACE SAYS OTHER-WISE...

ARIA'S BARMBRACK DIDN'T HAVE RINGS OR COINS.
AS LONG AS SHE STAYS HERE, SHE HAS NO NEED FOR WEALTH OR MARRIAGE.

KII (CREAK)
キィ…

I WONDER IF THOSE WERE LEFT OUT ON PURPOSE, TO KEEP HER FROM LONGING FOR THE OUTSIDE WORLD...
...WHEN SHE HAS NO CHOICE BUT TO STAY HERE IN SOLITUDE.
...

WHY DON'T WE DEAL WITH THE MAGIC BARRIER AT A LATER DATE?
OH!
RIGHT! THE MAGIC BARRIER!!

I SWEAR IT'S TRUE!! COLLEEN WAS THERE WITH ME!
SURE THING, HONEY.
NOW YOU HAVE AN EARLY MORNING TOMORROW, SO HURRY BACK TO YOUR ROOM.

YOU TOO, COLLIE. FINISH BRUSHING YOUR TEETH, AND THEN IT'S BEDTIME.
OKEY DOKEY.
TEKO (TRUP)
TEKO
TEKO
TEKO

MISS WITCH...
SHAKO (BRUSH)
SHAKO
UMMM ...
...HUH?
SHAKO
SHAKO
SHAKO

SHAKO SHAKO SHA
しゃこしゃこしゃ
I FORGOT TO ASK HER WHAT HER NAME WAS...
HATA (HALT)
はた…

WE'RE FRIENDS...
...AFTER ALL!

NIKOOO (SMIIILE)

にこーっ

COME BACK, OKAAAY!!?

IT'S FINE. I CAN ASK NEXT TIME!

ぺーっ

PEEE (PTOOEY)

END

~How to Make Nettle Tea~

Rinse the herbs you picked.
(Make sure you wear rubber gloves or something for the prickly hairs!)
ジャー
JAAA (VSHHH)
Drain the herbs and dry them out for two to three days.
They'll look dry and crispy.
(You can drink the tea without drying them!!)
Pour hot water in and let it steep for five minutes!!
It has a mild flavor much like green tea!! It can help alleviate allergies like hay fever.
You can add honey in to taste too!

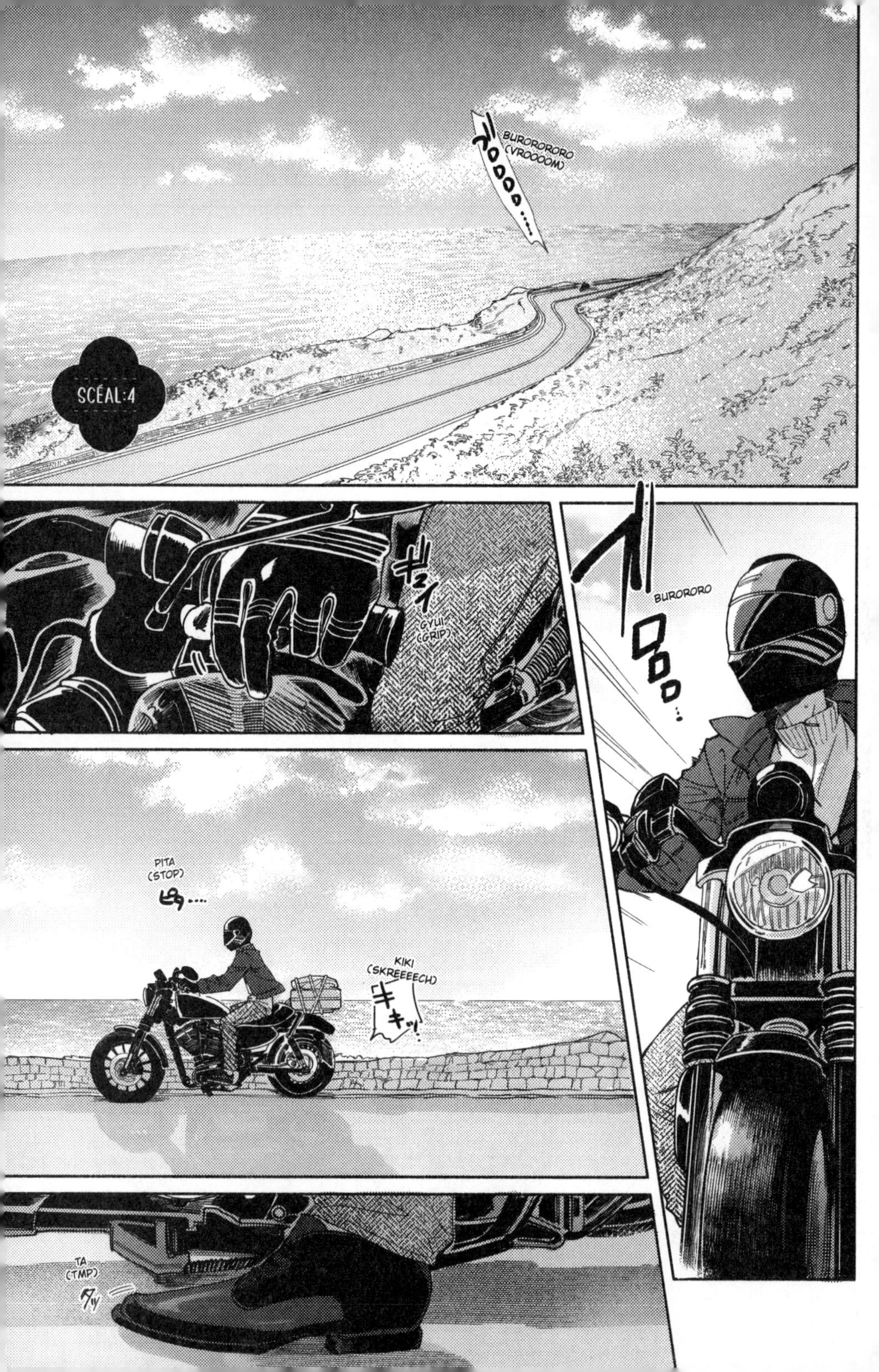

BURORORORO (VROOOOM)

SCÉAL:4

BURORORO

GYUI (GRIP)

KIKI (SKREEEECH)

PITA (STOP)

TA (TMP)

SO HOT!

I WONDER HOW ARIA'S DOING...

BOOO (TRANCE)
ぼーっ…
FUR
AH!
ばっ
BA (FWIP)
SO MUCH FUR...
HMM?
PACHIRI (BLINK)
ぱちり…
ぴく
PIKU (PRICK)

SCÉAL:4

しゃか
SHAKA (SCRUB)
もっ
MOFU (FLUFF)
もっ
MOFU
しゃか
SHAKA
もっ
MOFU
すぅーーっ
SUUUUUU (INHALE)
AWWWR...
AWWWWW...

GORON (FLOP)
ごろんっ
MRRR
OKAY! NEXT UP IS YOUR TUMMYYY!
MOFU
もっ…
COMPLETE SURRENDER...
'TIS THE SEASON FOR SOME GROOMING...
SHAKO
しゃこ
SHAKO
しゃこ
SHAKO
しゃこ

こんもり
KONMORI (HEAP)
I GOT SO MUCH...!
GWYN'S SHED FUR
WHAT'RE YOU GONNA DO WITH THAT FUR?
サッ
SA (SHF)
EH HEH HEH!
PAW!
サッ!
SA
ACK!

I COULDN'T HELP IT! I'VE BEEN CONDI-TIONED...!

HEE HEE...

OTHER PAW!

SHUPA (SHWIP)

しゅぱっ

WHA!?

ROLL OVER!

KURURIN (TWIRL)

くるりんっ

GORON (ROLL)

ごろんっ

GOOD BOOOY!
PACHI (CLAP)
ぱち
PACHI
ぱち
PACHI
ぱち
ZUUUN (DROOP)
ズーン…

SUN (POUT)
スンッ…
HUH!?
WHAT'S WRONG?
?
MY DIGNITY... I FEEL LIKE I'VE LOST ALL SORTS OF DIGNITY...

"DIG-NIT-TEE"? YOU'RE SO FUNNY, GWYN!
KERA
KERA (GIGGLE)
SO? WHAT ARE YOU DOING WITH MY FUR?
EH HEH HEH!
...
ZA (ZSH)
ARIA! COME ON!
ANSWER ME!
TA (TMP)
OH, HEY, WHAT SHOULD WE HAVE FOR DINNER TONIGHT?
TA
YOU ALWAYS DEFLECT WHEN IT'S INCONVENIENT FOR YOU!
IT'S A BAD HABIT, YOU KNOW.
EEK! STOP BITING MY CLOTHES!
!
SU (SLIP)
I'LL STOP WHEN YOU ANSWER ME!
GII (CREAK)
ARIA?

HATA (FREEZE)
はた…

HUH?
WHAT?
HOLY CRAP!!
ビクッ
BIKU (JOLT)

good friend!!
?
!?
SAFETY
EXPLAINING...

AH HA HA!
I SEE. A TALKING WOLF, HUH...?

YOU SCARED ME FOR A SECOND THERE—I THOUGHT ARIA WAS BEING ATTACKED BY A WOLF.
UH...
THIS GUY HERE COMES BY ONCE A MONTH. HIS NAME IS—
THEODORE! NICE TO MEET YA!
IT'S ALMOST SCARY HOW QUICKLY HE ACCEPTED MY EXISTENCE ...
OH, I THINK YOU MENTIONED HIM BEFORE, ARIA.
THE MERCHANT ...?
WHAT'S THIS!?
AWW, ARIA! YOU TOLD HIM ABOUT ME!?
GURI
GURI (NOOGIE)
HUH...? NO... I-IT JUST CAME UP...
YOU MAY GRUMBLE, BUT YOU'RE SUCH A LITTLE SWEETIE!

H... HEY... MY HEAD ...
HM?

NIYA
NIYA (SMIRK)
....
HMM?
YOU NEED TO SAY WHAT YOU'RE THINKING. I'M NOT A MIND READER, YOU KNOOOW!
GURI (NOOGIE)
GURI
GURI

M... MY HEAD...
GURI
GURI
YOU'LL... MESS UP...MY HAIR...
HMMMMMMM??
MUNYUUU (MOOSH)

I CAN'T HEEEAR YOUUU! ♪
NGH!
G...
NH!
GWYYYN!
JITABATA (FLAIL)
GURI
GURI
STILL IN A HUFF ABOUT EARLIER

WELL, HE MAY BE A STRANGE ONE...
...BUT IT'S NICE TO SEE ARIA DOES KNOW SOMEONE HUMAN...
GUGIGI (SQUEEZE)
...I MUST SAY, THOUGH...
A TALKING WOLF, HUH? NEVER SEEN ONE BEFORE.
JIII (STARE)

PAW!
ACK!
SHUTA (FWISH)
SU (SHF)
OTHER PAW!
SHUTATA

ARE YOU SERIOUS!? HOLY MOTHER OF ALL, YOU'RE SUCH A GOOD BOOOY!
BWAH HA HA HA!
COULDN'T HELP IT
I'M LOSING MY CONFIDENCE IN MYSELF AS A WOLF...
ZUUN (DROOP)
WOLF
WHY DOES EVERYONE KEEP TREATING ME LIKE A DOG...?

COME TO THINK OF IT, WE'VE NEVER MET BEFORE, HAVE WE?
EVEN THOUGH I'VE LIVED HERE FOR FOUR MONTHS NOW...
YEAH. I HATE THE COLD, SO I TOOK A WORK TRIP...
...TO A COUNTRY DOWN SOUTH...

AND THIS YEAR WAS WORSE THAN USUAL, THANKS TO A CERTAIN SOMEONE...
じっ...
JI (STARE)
IT WAS HER.
?

BUT I TRAVEL ALL OVER FOR WORK ANYWAY.
AND I DIDN'T NEED TO MAKE ANY PURCHASES YET, SO IT'S COOL.
"PURCHASES"?
YEP.

THE HERBS ARIA GROWS ARE HIGHLY SOUGHT-AFTER!

ZURARI (FULL)
ずらり

OKAY, SO DRY HERBS, THE USUAL MEDICINE, AND... DO YOU WANT THE TINCTURES TOO?
YEAH.
YOU SURE MADE A LOT.

SO YOU REALLY DO SELL THE STUFF ARIA MAKES.
YEP. SHE MAKES QUALITY PRODUCTS.

AND...
...CERTAIN ORGANIZATIONS WILL PAY TOP DOLLAR FOR ANYTHING MADE BY A WITCH...
'COS, YOU KNOW, THEY'RE PRACTICALLY AN ENDANGERED SPECIES...
...I THINK I'LL STAY AWAY FROM THIS TOPIC...
THESE "ORGANIZATIONS" SOUND DUBIOUS...

THERE'S QUITE A LOT HERE SINCE I DIDN'T COME IN THE WINTER, HUH?
KONMORI (HEAP)
こんもりっ

ARE YOU REALLY TAKING THAT MUCH?

IT LOOKED LIKE YOU CAME BY MOTORCYCLE.

WILL IT ALL FIT IN YOUR BAG??

CONSIDERABLY MORE THAN THE SIZE OF HIS BAG

OH...

NO PROBLEM.

HUP!

HYOI (WHOOP)
ひょい
HYOI
ひょいい
HYOI
ひょいっ
?
HUP!
UH...!
HYOI
ひょいい
WHERE EXACTLY IS IT ALL GOING...?
HYOI
ひょいい
HYOI
ひょいっ
???
DON (WHAM)
ドンッ!

OH, RIGHT. I'M IN A WITCH'S HOUSE...
ALL RIGHTY! EVERYTHING'S PUT AWAY.
GACHA (CLICK)
I FORGOT BECAUSE I'VE NEVER SEEN ARIA USE HER POWERS...
SO IF YOU CAN USE MAGIC ...
...DOES THAT MEAN YOU'RE A WIZARD?
THAT IS MAGIC, ISN'T IT?
OH! I FORGOT TO MENTION...
...I'M GANIEDA'S—
ARIA'S GRANDMOTHER'S SON, SO YEAH!
I'M GOOD AT MAGIC.
I EVEN MADE THIS MAGIC BAG MYSELF!
WHAT !!?
ALTHOUGH, ARIA WAS ADOPTED, AND I'M NOT MUCH DIFFERENT ...
...SO NONE OF US ARE BLOOD RELATED.
AH... I SEE...

BUT ARIA'S LIKE A DAUGHTER OR LITTLE SISTER TO ME. I CAN'T HELP BUT FAWN OVER HER...

LOOK AT YOU! SO CUUUTE!

SHE'S NOT ENJOYING IT ONE BIT...

PURAAAN (LIIIMP)

ぷら〜〜ん

MUSU (POUT)

ムスッ

YOU...

...DON'T SEEM VERY SURPRISED TO HEAR THAT ARIA'S ADOPTED...

SU (SLIP)

すっ

UH... IT'S NOT THAT RARE...

DOES HE NOT TRUST ME?

HMM?
......BY THE WAY, IT'S A LITTLE LATE TO ASK, BUT...
...DIDN'T GANIEDA PUT A MAGIC BARRIER AROUND THIS PLACE? HOW DID THIS WOLF WANDER IN?
ギクッ!!
GIKU (GULP)

......AHH, I GET IT...
AND NOW THOSE NEIGHBOR-HOOD KIDS KNOW WITCHES EXIST, HUH?
しゅん……
SHUN (GLUM)
I'M SORRY. I BROKE THE RULES...
HUH? IT'S FINE, ISN'T IT?
ケロリ
KERORI (FLIPPANT)
ジトッ…
JITO (GLARE)
ズ…
ZU (SIP)
WHAT'S WITH THE EYES...? FYI, I WASN'T JUST SAYING IT OFFHANDEDLY. I MEAN IT.
WELL, IF YOU REALLY NEED IT, I CAN FIX THE BARRIER FOR YOU.
ACK! HOT!
HUH?
I'M PRETTY SURE I CAN FIGURE OUT HOW TO PUT ONE UP.
IS THE TEA REALLY THAT HOT?

WHAAAT? YOU DON'T TRUST MY SKILLS?
I MEAN, NATURALLY IT WON'T BE AS GOOD AS GANIEDA'S, BUT STILL...
SORO (SLOW)
CHIRO (LICK)
N-NO. THAT'S NOT IT...
AFTER WE REALIZED WHAT HAPPENED, I TRIED PUTTING ONE UP MYSELF...
IT WAS MY FIRST TIME...
...SO I DON'T KNOW IF IT WORKED...
...BUT, WELL, EVEN IF...IT DIDN'T...
...UM...

'KAY.

KOTO (TUNK) コトッ

WELL, IF YOU SAY SO.

...THOUGH YOU HAVE PLENTY TO MAKE ME WORRY ABOUT...

HERE. TAKE THIS.

SU (SLIP) すっ…

? PAPER?

IT'S SHAPED LIKE A BIRD...

IF THAT ONE STARTS TRYING TO EAT YOU, LET ME KNOW RIGHT AWAY.

ANYTHING HAPPENS AND THAT BIRD WILL COME FLYING TO ME.

I'LL COME AGAIN SOON.
GREAT SEEING YOU AGAIN, MY DEAR, SWEET ARIA!
EASY DOES IT!
MUCHUUU (SMOOCH)
ムチュ〜ッ
...
GESSORI (HAGGARD)
げっそり…
CAN'T BE BOTHERED TO REACT ANYMORE

HUMANS ARE SELF-SERVING, ATTENTION-SEEKING DEMONS...
THEY GET JEALOUS 'COS I'M HOT AND HAVE A TON OF INSTAGROM FOLLOWERS, SO THEY TROLL ME ALL THE TIME.
HAAAAAAH...
I'M SO SICK OF THE OUTSIDE WORLD...
OH...
"INS-TUH-GROHM FOWELERS"...? MUST BE HARD OUT THERE... I GUESS???
NYA HA HA!
"A TENSION-SEEKING"
HE MUST BE WHY ARIA NEVER WANTS TO GO OUT...

……
IS THE OUTSIDE WORLD REALLY THAT TOUGH?

OH! UM...
DON'T TAKE ME TOO SERIOUSLY......
BUN (WAVE) BUN
......
WELL, SURE, THERE'S PLENTY OF BAD STUFF OUTSIDE...
...BUT THERE ARE SO MANY FUN THINGS THAT MAKE UP FOR IT.
I ACTUALLY DON'T MIND LIVING OUT THERE.
PON (PAT)
ぽんっ

IF ANYTHING HAPPENS TO YOU, I'LL RUSH TO YOUR SIDE.
AND IF YOU EVER WANT TO DO ANYTHING, I'LL HELP YOU FIGURE IT OUT.
FOR NOW, JUST FOLLOW YOUR HEART.

...THANKS.

TAKE CARE!
I'LL MAKE SURE TO COME BY SOONER NEXT TIME!

THE WIND'S STARTING TO GET COLD.

LET'S LOCK UP AFTER WE PUT ALL THIS AWAY.

KACHA (CLINK)

RIGHT!

...

GWYN, DO YOU KNOW WHAT "INS-TUH-GROHM FOWELERS" ARE?
ERRR...
AHHH... I CAN'T SAY I DO...

I WONDER IF IT'S REALLY THAT FUN...

MAYBE YOU SHOULD ASK NEXT TIME HE COMES.
UH-HUH...

I'M SURE HE'LL BE BACK AGAIN SOON.
UH-HUH...

OH! UM...
NOT THAT I WANT HIM TO!
FUKI (WIPE)
SA (SHF)
FUKI
WELL, YEAH, IT'S HELPFUL WHEN HE BRINGS US A BUNCH OF STUFF, BUT STILL!
THERE SHE GOES AGAIN.

THOUGH, HONESTLY, I'M A BIT RELIEVED.
ABOUT WHAT?
OH, YOU KNOW. YOU'RE SUCH A SHY GIRL, ARIA...
...SO I THOUGHT YOU'D NEVER SPOKEN TO ANYONE BUT YOUR GRAND-MOTHER.
...
NO ILL WILL

AND IT'S NICE TO KNOW YOU HAVE A HUMAN GUARDIAN LIKE THAT.
WHAT ARE YOU TALKING ABOUT ...?
GACHA (KACHAK)
ガチャ

HE KEEPS CLAIMING HE'S HER SON...
...BUT THAT GUY'S A CAT-SITH, GWYN.
Cat-Sith
A feline fairy said to appear mainly in the form of a black cat. Some hide in people's homes, some are capable of speaking, and some walk on two feet. There are many versions of a cat-sith.

WHAT!?
A FAIRY...?
MEOOOW

CAT
FAIRY

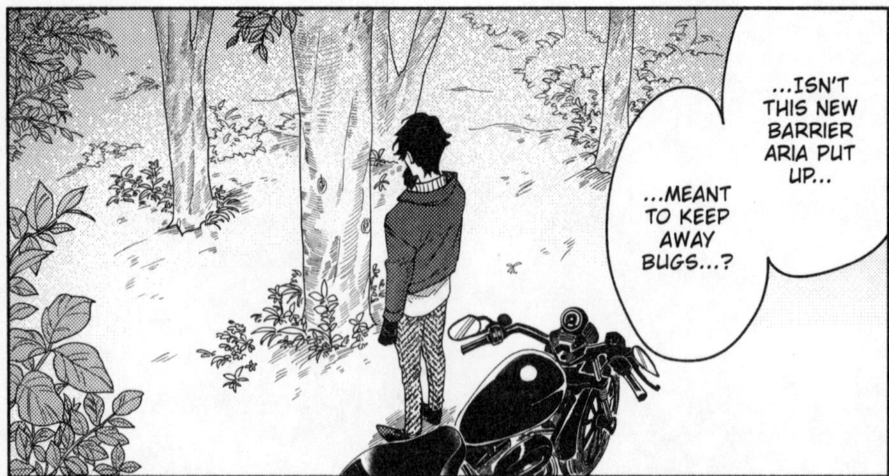
...ISN'T THIS NEW BARRIER ARIA PUT UP...
...MEANT TO KEEP AWAY BUGS...?

END

SCÉAL:5

AFTER FOUR MONTHS OF LIVING HERE...
...GWYN STILL HADN'T SEEN ARIA USE ANY OF HER MAGIC.
KYU (CINCH)
きゅ
ZURARI (SHEBANG)
PREPARING LUNCH...

LOTS OF INGREDIENTS TODAY, HUH?
WHAT ARE YOU MAKING?
IT'S A SURPRISE! YOU'LL KNOW WHEN IT'S DONE.
LET'S START WITH THE SOUP.
MELT BUTTER IN SKILLET.
JUUU (SIZZZZ)
DICE ONIONS.
TON (CHOP)
TON
ADD TO MELTED BUTTER AND STIR-FRY TILL PARTIALLY SEE-THROUGH.
SPRINKLE IN MINCED LOVAGE AND FLOUR AND MIX.
LASTLY, ADD BOUILLON A LITTLE AT A TIME.
PACHI (CRACKLE)
JUUU

GUTSU (BLUB)
GUTSU
REDUCE HEAT AND ADD LID. BOIL IT DOWN...
PACHI
PACHI (CRACKLE)
...ADD MILK, MIX, AND VOILÀ!
PLACE A LAVENDER LEAF ON TOP, AND YOU'RE DONE!
YOU'RE COOKING LEEKS NEXT?
YUP.
CUT BOTH ENDS OF LEEK.
THEN CUT IN HALF LENGTHWISE.
MELT BUTTER AND ADD SLICED GARLIC.
JUUU (SIZZZZ)
PACHI
PLACE LEEKS CUT SIDE DOWN AND SAUTÉ UNTIL BROWNED.
PACHI
JUUU
FLIP LEEKS OVER AND SAUTÉ AGAIN. ADD WINE AND PUT ON LOW HEAT.
GUTSU
GUTSU
COVER AND LET SIMMER FOR THIRTY MINUTES.

LAST BUT NOT LEAST, POTA-TOOOES!
PEEL POTATOES AND PARBOIL.
REMOVE LID ONCE LEEKS ARE SOFT AND TENDER.
MUWA (STEAM)
SIMMER UNTIL ONLY HALF OF THE LIQUID IS LEFT.
PLATE AND TOP WITH PARSLEY, THYME, AND SHREDDED CHEESE.
SFX: SHAKO (GRATE) SHAKO
MASH HALF THE POTATOES UNTIL SMOOTH.
KAKO (MIX)
KAKO
GRATE REMAINING POTATOES.
WRING OUT AS MUCH LIQUID AS YOU CAN...
GUGUGU (STRAIN)
GYUUUU (SQUEEEEZE)
TOPOPO (KLUBLUB)
ADD CAKE FLOUR AND SALT AND STIR WELL. IF MIXTURE IS TOO THICK, ADJUST BY ADDING MILK OR THE LIKE.
...AND COMBINE IT WITH MASHED POTATOES. STIR WELL, AND YOUR BATTER IS DONE!

MELT THE BUTTER IN A SKILLET AND POUR THE BATTER IN.

じゅううう〜〜っ

JUUUU (SIZZZZ)

FRY UNTIL BOTTOM IS NICELY BROWNED AND FLIP THEM OVER. ENJOY!

くるっ

KURU (FLIP)

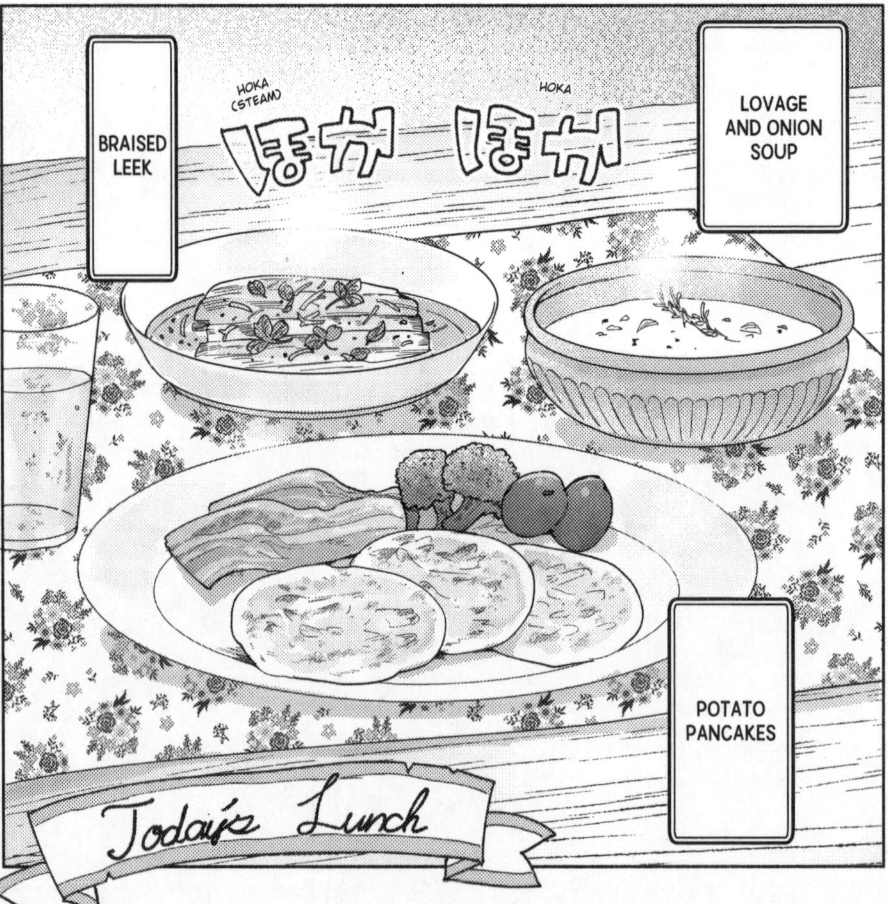

LOVAGE AND ONION SOUP

ほか ほか

HOKA (STEAM)

HOKA

BRAISED LEEK

POTATO PANCAKES

Today's Lunch

WOW! IT LOOKS DELICIOUS!
PAA (BEAM)
...D-DOES IT?
UH-HUH! IT SMELLS AMAZING.
YOU'RE ALWAYS SO OVER-THE-TOP, GWYN.
THIS IS JUST YOUR BORING, EVERYDAY MEAL...
HERE'S YOUR WATER.
TOPOPO (KLUBLUB)
YOU THINK SO?
PFFT...
YOUR COOKING'S SO GOOD, ARIA. I CAN NEVER WAIT TO EAT IT.
O-OKAY, I GET IT...

NO, SERIOUSLY. YOU AKE DIFFERENT THINGS VERY DAY, AND YOU HAVE UCH A RICH REPERTOIRE. YOU PUT SUCH DETAILED OVE AND CARE INTO EVEN THE SIMPLE DISHES, SO THEY'RE PACKED WITH FLAVOR. PLUS, YOUR ESSERTS ARE YUMMY TOO! THAT CAKE YOU MADE THE OTHER DAY WAS TO DIE FOR, AND—

H-HURRY UP AND EAT, OR IT'LL ALL GET COOOLD!

BAN (SLAM)

I KEEP GETTING CARRIED AWAY BECAUSE OF HER CUTE REACTIONS...

REIN IT IN, GWYN.

HERE I GO!

CHIRO (LICK)

OH HEY, THE ONION SOUP TASTES A BIT DIFFERENT FROM HOW IT USUALLY DOES.

IT HAS A UNIQUE KICK TO IT...

IS THIS AN HERB TOO?

YEAH. I TRIED ADDING LOVAGE TODAY.

LOVAGE

Looks like celery but with a more intense smell and flavor. Good for the digestive system and allergies, and has several other benefits. Some say, long ago, lovage seeds were used as an aphrodisiac.

I CAN PICTURE YOU EATING VENISON...
HOW ABOUT RATS?
HUH...!? NUH-UH. I'M NOT ONE FOR DISGUSTING FOOD LIKE THAT...
GENNARI (QUEASY)
BUT YOU'RE A WOLF...
PAKU (NOM)

KACHA (CLINK)
WOLVES AREN'T ACTUALLY SUPPOSED TO EAT ONIONS, YOU KNOW...

WHAT DO YOU EAT BESIDES PEOPLE FOOD, GWYN?

SPEAK-ING OF...
ARIA'S A WITCH, YET SHE HARDLY USES MAGIC...
PAKU
HAMU (CHEW)
HAMU
I KNOW SHE'S USED IT A COUPLE TIMES IN THE PAST, BUT...
...IT WASN'T VERY CLEAR WHAT SHE DID.

ALTHOUGH... PERHAPS NOT ALL WITCHES CAN ACTUALLY USE MAGIC.
MAYBE SHE'S JUST CALLED ONE BECAUSE SHE MAKES MEDICINE...
?
WHAT?
MOKYU
MOKYU (MUNCH)
OH, NOTHING.

IT'S JUST REALLY CLEAR YOU'RE ENJOYING YOUR MEAL.
YOU'RE ADORABLE, ARIA.
NGH!
......GWYN, YOU...
?
....
...?
URGH...
NEVER MIND...
HUH? JUST TELL ME.
PO (PLIP)
ぽつ
PO
ぽつ...

OH NO!!
I SHOULD BRING IN THOSE TOWELS I PUT OUT TO DRY.
GATA (CLATTER)
BA (JUMP)
I'LL HELP TOO.
DON'T!
IT'S A PAIN TO WASH YOU WHEN YOU GET ALL MUDDY. YOU STAY THERE!
PATA PATA (PITTER)
I MEAN, SHE'S RIGHT, BUT STILL...
ZAAAAA (VSHHH)
IT'S COMING DOWN HARD.
I HOPE SHE'S OKAY OUT THERE.

OH NO, YOU'RE SOAKING WET!
ARE YOU ALL RIGHT!?
NH...
ぴょんっ
PYON (LEAP)
AH! OF COURSE NOT.
BISSHORI (DRENCHED)
びっしょり…
POTA (DRIP)
ぽた…
POTA
ぽた
HERE'S A TOWEL. TAKE OFF THOSE CLOTHES AND DRY UP.
WE SHOULD GET A FIRE GOING TOO. LET'S SEE, THE LOGS ARE...
POTA
ポタ
ポタ
POTA
POTA
ポタッ
ぴちゃん
PICHAN (PLOP)

TO THINK WE'D HAVE A LEAK NOW...
POTA
ぽた
POTA
ぽた
THE LOGS GOT ALL WET...
MAYBE WE CAN STILL USE THE ONES AT THE BOTTOM?
SU (SLIP)
すっ
RELAX, GWYN.
SURU (TUG)
するっ
WHO DO YOU THINK I AM?

UH... YOU'RE ARIA.

I'M A WITCH, REMEMBER!?

KUWA (GLARE)

BA (LUNGE)

OH! THAT'S WHAT YOU MEANT.

I DON'T NEED LOGS. IT'S JUST STARTING A FIRE. I CAN DO IT WITH MAGIC...

CHOI (WAVE) CHOI

SHIIIN (HUSHHH)

すくっ
SUKU (STAND)
ぱたん
PATAN (SHUT)
CHOI
ちょい
しーん…
SHIIIN
ちょい
CHOI
ちょい
CHOI

BUT MAGIC DOES EXIST IN THIS WORLD. I KNOW THAT FOR CERTAIN.

OTHERWISE, I WOULDN'T BE IN THIS FORM.

AND ARIA'S GRAND-MOTHER...

CHIKA (SPARK)
HM?
!?
BON (BOOM)
WHA...?
WHAT WAS THAT !?
I HEARD A HUGE SOUND...
BA (RUSH)
PUSHUUU (FSSHHHH)
WHAT ...?
BURNED TO A CRISP...

た....
は
HATA (HALT)

PFFT!
HA-HA-HA-HA-HA-HA-HA!
YOU'RE ALL BLACK, GWYN!!
HA-HA...
HUH!?

I JUMPED AT THAT HUGE SOUND, BUT...
...DID YOU DIVE INTO THE FIREPLACE OR WHAT?
ぷす
PUSU (FSHHH)
UH, WELL...
ぷす...
PUSU

HEE HEE!
OH, GWYN! WHAT WERE YOU THINKING!?
IT'S GONNA BE A REAL PAIN TO CLEAN THIS!

SORRY ...
I SWEAR I SAW FIRE...

ZAAA (VSHHH)
ザザ――ッ…

IT'S SO HARD TO GET THE CHARCOAL OFF 'COS YOUR FUR'S SO WHITE.
GOSHI (RUB)
GOSHI

YOU KNOW ...
...I NOTICED YOU MADE MORE PANCAKES THAN USUAL TODAY.
GIKU (GULP)
ギクッ

IT WAS FOR THEM, RIGHT?
I WONDER WHEN THOSE TWO WILL BE BACK.
SHAKO (SCRUB)
SHAKO
...WHO CARES?

YOU'RE ALL I NEED, GWYN.
...
SHAKO (SCRUB) しゃこ

NOW I'VE DONE IT.
I DIDN'T REALIZE IT WAS A SORE SPOT FOR HER...
SHAKO
BUT THAT FIRE...
ZAAA (VSHHH)
WAS THE BLIZZARD THAT DAY ALSO...?
I MEAN...
...IS THAT EVEN POSSIBLE?

END

FUKI
フキ
FUKI
(WIPE)
フキ

SCÉAL:6
I DON'T HAVE MUCH TIME LEFT IN THIS WORLD.

I'M SURE IT'LL CAUSE HER PLENTY OF PAIN AND SORROW.
BUT THIS IS THE ONLY WAY I CAN PROTECT HER... BY ISOLATING HER FROM THE OUTSIDE.
SURI (STROKE)
IF...

IF YOU SUCCEED IN YOUR GOAL...
...AND ARE WILLING TO COME BACK HERE...
...WOULD YOU PLEASE LOOK AFTER ARIA...?
!
GWYN.
もぞ…
MOZO (SNUGGLE)
ぱち
PACHI (BLINK)

GWYN...
RISE AND SHINE!
I ALREADY MADE BREAK-FAST.
YOU'RE USUALLY UP BEFORE ME. HOW OUT OF CHAR-ACTER.
WHAT A NOS-TALGIC DREAM...
MOSO (RUSTLE)
もそ
MUKURI (RISE)
MM...
KUN (SNIFF)
KUN
SMELLS NICE...
I MADE OMELETS TODAY.
TON (TONK)
TON
NOSO (DRAG)
NOSO

Irish Omelet
There are mashed potatoes inside of it!
TIME TO EAT!
モグッ
MOGU (NOM)
LOOKS
YUMMY...
YOU LIKE IT?
YEAH!
ニコッ!
NIKO (GRIN)
I GET TO EAT AMAZING BREAKFASTS WITH ARIA EVERY MORNING...
モグ
MOGU
Boxty
Stew
Soda bread
モキュ
MOKYU (MUNCH)
Colcannon
...AND I'M IN BLISS. I REALLY AM...
モグ
MOGU
...BUT IT'S JUST...
むく
MUKU
むく
MUKU (PLUMP)
HOW DO I EXPLAIN THIS...?
OH, I KNOW.

I FEEL LIKE A PARENT WHO CAN'T LET GO OF THEIR DAUGHTER...
EVEN THINKING ABOUT IT NOW TEARS MY HEART OUT...
モキュ
MOKYU (MUNCH)
MMM... ♥
モキュ
MOKYU

I WONDER IF ALL DADS FEEL THIS WAY WHEN EATING BREAKFAST WITH THEIR DAUGH-TERS...
ペロ
PERO
ペロッ
PERO (LICK)
YOU'RE DRINKING A LOT OF WATER.
GWYN, DO YOU WANT A REFILL?
YES, PLEASE.

コキュッ
KOKYU (SQUEAK)
...REALLY, THOUGH.

YOU'RE SO BIG NOW...

"BIG" ...?
UH...! I MEAN...
NO...
HOW SHOULD I INTERPRET THAT!?
AND THE LOOK ON HER FACE AS SHE GIVES IT TO ME...
W-WANT HALF OF... MY OMELET?
SU (SLIDE)
HUH? YOU DON'T WANT IT?

WELL, YOU'RE NOT WRONG...
I'VE BEEN THINKING ABOUT MY DIET TOO...
NOW I GET IT!
OH! OHHH!!
THAT'S NOT WHAT I MEANT AT ALL...

BUT HEY, GIRLS TEND TO BE CUTER WHEN THEY HAVE A LITTLE MEAT ON THEM!
PISHI (SNAP)

ZAWA (SWISH)
WELL, AT THE END OF THE DAY, YOU KNOW!
EXERCISE IS THE BEST WAY TO LOSE WEIGHT!
MUSU (SULK)
TOKO (TMP)
TOKO

YOU DON'T GET GIRLS AT ALL, GWYN.
SOME-TIMES YOU SAY HURTFUL STUFF.
PUSUUU (POUT)
I'LL WATCH MY WORDS...
SORRY...
AND THIS IS HOW CLUELESS IT FEELS TO BE A DAD...

WAS YOUR LAST OWNER NOT A GIRL?

OH YEAH. ARIA THINKS I WAS A PET...

IT WASN'T MY OWNER, BUT...

TOTE (TRUP)

TOTE

WELL, SHE WAS A WOMAN, BUT...

...SHE WAS A BIT DETACHED COMPARED TO YOUR AVERAGE PERSON...

HMM ...?

...
I'D RATHER DIE THAN GO BACK.
TH- THAT BAD?
IT MUST HAVE BEEN HELL...
DO YOU EVER WANT TO GO BACK TO YOUR OLD HO—
NEVER.
LIKE I SAID BEFORE, I DON'T HAVE A PLACE TO CALL HOME—
ASIDE FROM HERE, THAT IS.
...I SEE.

DA (SHOOM)
GWYN!
?
C'MON...
RACE YA!
SHE CHEERED UP..?

DA (SHOOM)
PYUUU (ZWOOSH)
YOU'RE SO FAST!
HEH HEH
DON'T UNDER-ESTIMATE THE SPEED OF A FOUR-LEGGED ANIMAL.
NOT FAIR!
GWYYYN! AT LEAST RUN ON TWO LEGS INSTEAD OF FOUR!
THAT'S A PRETTY TALL ORDER.
HEY! WAIT UP!
AH HA HA!,
GWYYYN!

HAAH.
UGH. WHAT'S WITH THIS NEVER-ENDING PILE OF WORK...?
I JUST WANT TO GET THIS DONE AND GO HOME...
BUUU (VRRR)
HMM?
AN INSTA-GROM NOTIF ...?
DIDN'T I HAVE THESE OFF?
OH, AND IT'S JUST A POST FROM THEODORE ...
THAT DOSSER! ALWAYS GOOFING OFF WHEN HE HAS WORK TO DO...
HAAH...

1328 likes
...
WHOA!
ガチャッ
GACHA (KACHAK)
VICE PRESI-DENT!
ARE YOU HEADING OFF SOME-WHERE?
YEAH. IT'S URGENT.
スタ
SUTA (STRIDE)
I'LL READY A CAR—
スタ
SUTA
DON'T NEED IT!
THEN PLEASE, AT LEAST TELL ME WHERE YOU'RE GOING...

TO IRELAND.
IRELAND...?
ZAA (WHOOSH)
MR. WOLF, I...

...HAVE NOTHING BUT FEAR FOR HUMANS.
THEY TOOK MY BELOVED FROM ME...
KOTE (TRIP)
...AND I CAN NO LONGER LIVE ANY OTHER WAY.

THAT SAID, I WANT THIS GIRL TO HAVE A BRIGHT FUTURE...
FU (WHISH)
HFF!
HFF!
...AND SO I CAN'T HELP BUT HOPE THEY'LL DO BETTER BY HER.
BUWA (WHOOSH)

ZA
(SHF)
SUKU
(LIFT)
HFF!
HFF!
HFF!
HFF!

HFF!
ザリ
ZARI (CRUNCH)
HFF!
I PRAY...
...WITH EVERY FIBER OF MY BEING...
HFF!
HAAAH...

...THAT HER FUTURE IS FULL OF PEACE—

I'VE NEVER COME THIS FAR OUT BEFORE...

I HEARD EVERYONE ON THE OUTSIDE IS MEAN LIKE THEODORE...
...AND THAT I SHOULD NEVER LEAVE THE BARRIER.
THEO-DORE, HUH...?
...

IT'S SO PRETTY.
IT IS.
GASA (RUSTLE)
ARIA...

LOOKS LIKE WE HAVE COMPANY.

END

MIGHT AS WELL
TAKE ONE!!!
?

Aria of the Beech Forest

WILL CONTINUE IN VOLUME 2

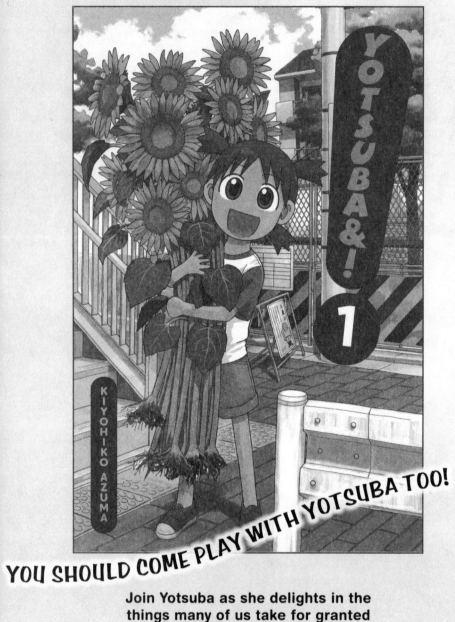

Hello! This is YOTSUBA!
Guess what? Guess what?
Yotsuba and Daddy just moved here
from waaaay over there!
And Yotsuba met these
nice people next door and made
new friends to play with!
The pretty one took
Yotsuba on a bike ride!
(Whoooa! There was a big hill!)
And Ena's a good drawer!
(Almost as good as Yotsuba!)
And their mom always
gives Yotsuba ice cream!
(Yummy!)
And...
And...
OHHHH!

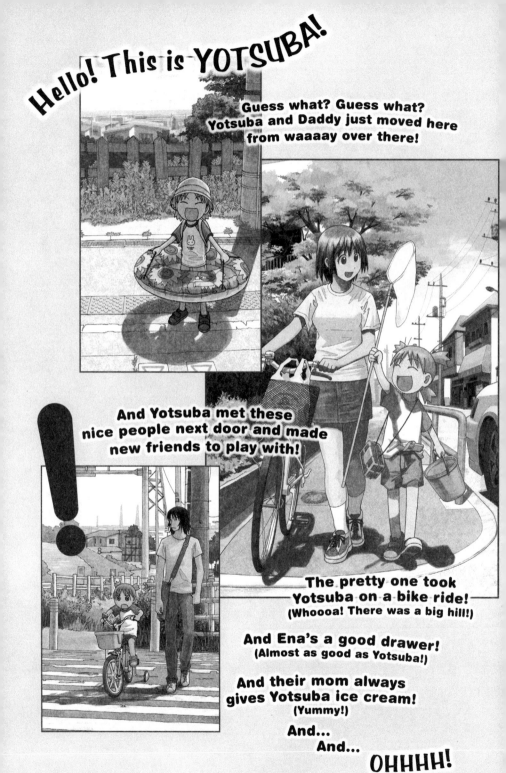

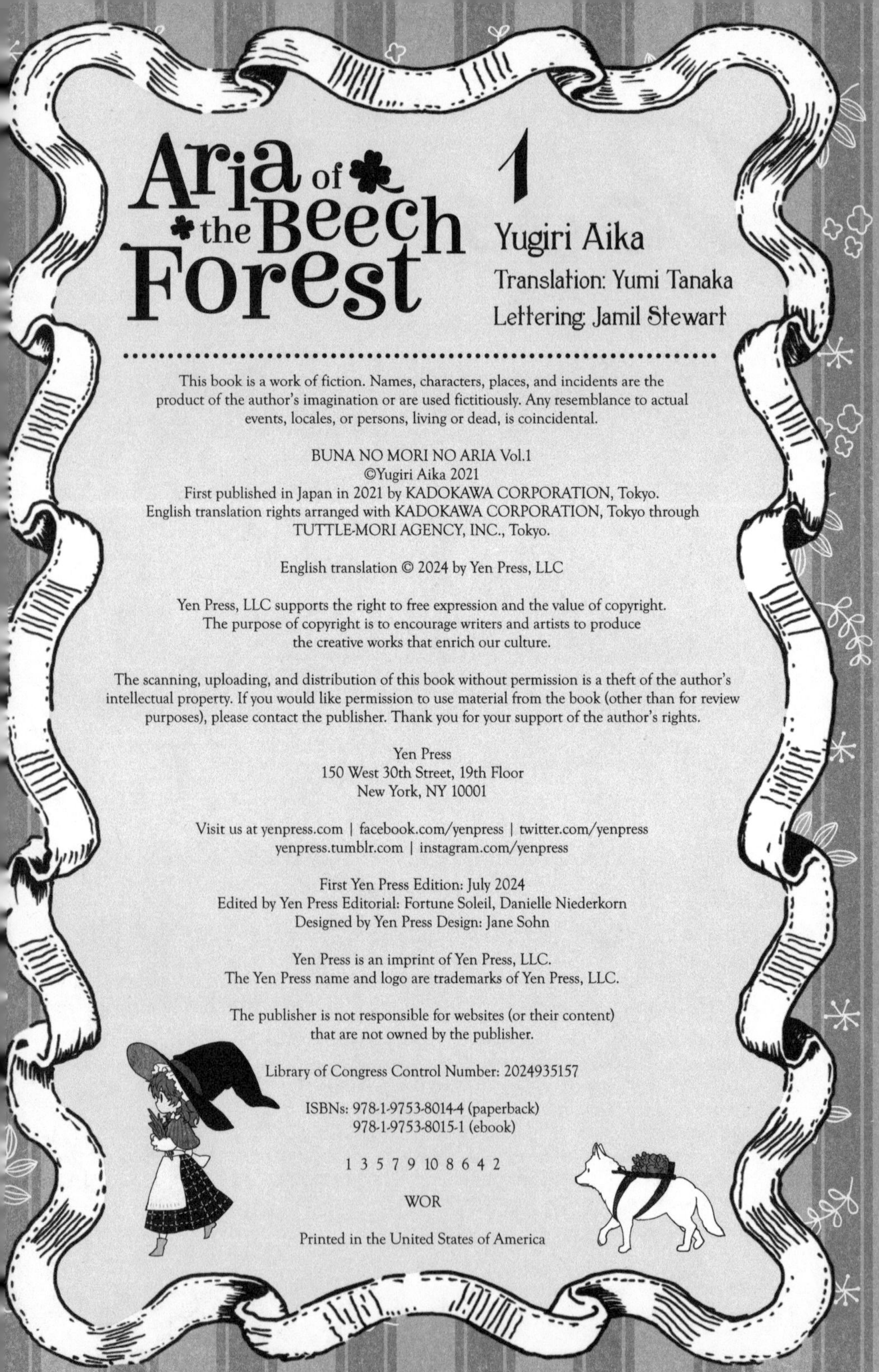

Aria of the Beech Forest 1

Yugiri Aika

Translation: Yumi Tanaka

Lettering: Jamil Stewart

BUNA NO MORI NO ARIA Vol.1

First published in Japan in 2021 by KADOKAWA CORPORATION, Tokyo.
English translation rights arranged with KADOKAWA CORPORATION, Tokyo through TUTTLE-MORI AGENCY, INC., Tokyo.

Yen Press
150 West 30th Street, 19th Floor
New York, NY 10001

Visit us at yenpress.com | facebook.com/yenpress | twitter.com/yenpress
yenpress.tumblr.com | instagram.com/yenpress

First Yen Press Edition: July 2024
Edited by Yen Press Editorial: Fortune Soleil, Danielle Niederkorn
Designed by Yen Press Design: Jane Sohn

Yen Press is an imprint of Yen Press, LLC.
The Yen Press name and logo are trademarks of Yen Press, LLC.

The publisher is not responsible for websites (or their content) that are not owned by the publisher.

Library of Congress Control Number: 2024935157

ISBNs: 978-1-9753-8014-4 (paperback)
978-1-9753-8015-1 (ebook)

1 3 5 7 9 10 8 6 4 2

WOR

Printed in the United States of America